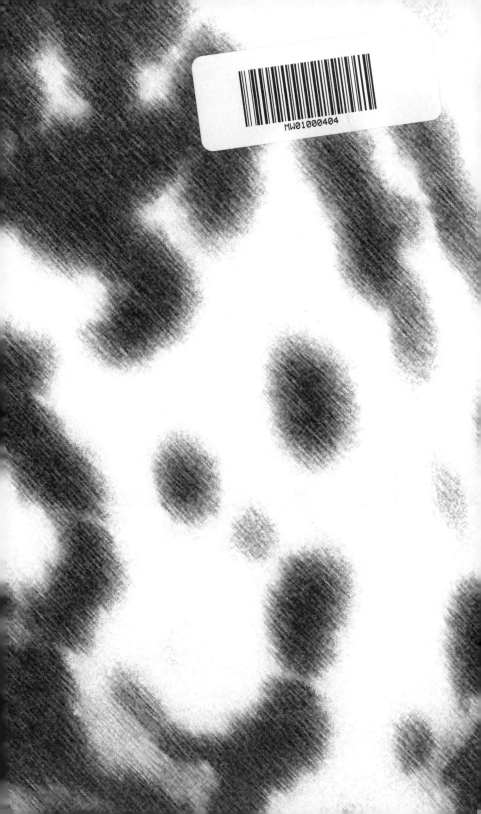

MW01000404

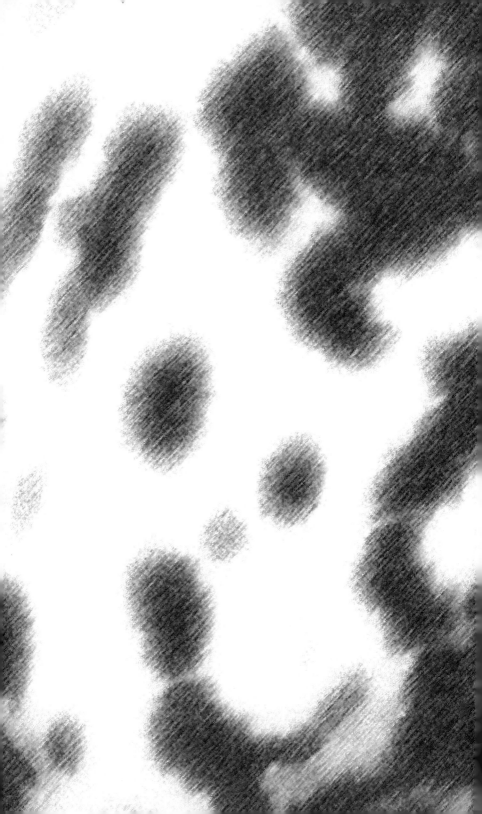

ALSO AVAILABLE FROM CITY LIGHTS/SISTER SPIT

Sister Spit: Writing, Rants and Reminiscence from the Road
Edited by Michelle Tea

Cha Ching!
By Ali Liebegott

FORTHCOMING:

Yokohama Threeway
By Beth Lisick

THE BEAUTIFULLY WORTHLESS

THE
BEAUTIFULLY
WORTHLESS

Ali Liebegott

San Francisco

ACKNOWLEDGMENTS
Portions of *The Beautifully Worthless* were inspired by the poems of Pablo Neruda, Christopher Smart, Dante, Emily Dickinson, Adrienne Rich, and Larry Levis. Thanks to Greg Wharton and Ian Phillips for first publishing this manuscript in 2005 on Suspect Thoughts Press. Deep gratitude goes to City Lights/Sister Spit Press and Michelle Tea for giving this book another life. Parts of this manuscript first appeared in *Lodestar Quarterly, Bloom, Solo, Art/Life, and Blood and Tears: Poems for Matthew Shepard.* Thank you Beth Pickens, for all your love and support.

Library of Congress Cataloging-in-Publication Data

Liebegott, Ali.
  [Poems. Selections]
  The beautifully worthless / Ali Liebegott.
     pages cm. — (City lights/sister spit)
  ISBN 978-0-87286-571-6
  1. Young women—Poetry. 2. Lesbians—Poetry. 3. Women travelers
—Poetry. 4. Waitresses—Poetry. I. Title.

  PS3612.I327B43 2013
  811'.6—dc23

                        2012044098

City Lights Books are published at the City Lights Bookstore
261 Columbus Avenue, San Francisco, CA 94133
www.citylights.com

In memory of Deborah Digges
and Adrienne Rich
and Rorschach
R.I.P.

BROOKLYN TO CAMUS

But you were young, and you had
Plenty of time:
Going west,

You slept with your mouth open.
You were nothing,
You were snow falling through the ribs
of the dead.

You were all I had.

—Larry Levis, from "The Spirit Says, You Are Nothing"

Sometime in October

When I packed up the old place I didn't want to throw anything out because I wasn't sure where my birth certificate was and I didn't have time to look for it—so I dumped everything into boxes, trash bags and pillowcases. The matchbooks and pennies came from shaking the top drawer of a kitchen cabinet into a box. When I lived in Yonkers and was the brokest I've ever been in my life, those pennies saved me a couple times—bought me coffee at 7-11, and once I didn't have enough pennies on my lunch break from the pet supply store to get a kid's burger at McDonald's, so I hid in the warehouse behind the stacks of kitty litter and ate the staff donuts. By the third jelly donut my head was spinning. The rest of my boxes were filled with eighty percent trash—dirty Q-tips and coffee-stained napkins. There were matchbooks from bars I had gone to five years and 3,000 miles ago. Everything I own could fit in the back of a pickup truck, but three out of ten boxes are filled with matchbooks and dirty Q-tips. I want things to be different in this apartment, but I don't know where to begin. So for now, I dumped all the matchbooks and pennies in a duffel bag and put it under the bed.

Still October, Still Sad

I can't stop dwelling on the fact that I moved a box filled with matchbooks and pennies. I wrote down on a slip of paper, "matchbooks, pennies" and hung it on the wall so I wouldn't forget that I packed up the trash in my life and moved it with me to a new apartment. I could knit a sweater out of all the dog hair on the floor. Once my nonsmoking art teacher told me one of her students painted the most beautiful ashtray. She said, "Now someone who can make an ashtray look beautiful is a talented artist."

One Year Later

I had to take everything off my walls, all the newspaper clippings about people being bitten to death by rats and cures for gay dogs. I pulled down the paper that said, "matchbooks, pennies" too. I'll do anything to stop being depressed. I could be like those people who build bombs out of horseshit and plastic pipes. The women in jail told me how they light their cigarettes off the spark from rubbing a Brillo pad on a battery. And when a child gets trapped under a car, there's always a frail mother powered by frantic adrenaline who manages to lift the car off the ground with her bare hands. People fight diseases every day. Who gets to live a happy life, who gets born with a brain that works, it's so random, right? You're either destined to be a heroin addict or an accountant—you can't predict or prepare for life.

I wish somewhere buried under feet and feet of dirt
answers for the unanswerable slept safe and unharmed
just as the heart of the penny dangles, drunk and teeming
unnoticed to most, inside the copper-green edges of its
        decomposition.

And I wish one night I could dream the name of this town
where dirt shrines hope for the desperate,
where the pine-needled ground shifts and fidgets—
this place that has waited years for me to plunge
the straightedge of a spade into its dirt belly
and birth the gifts it has kept so long.

And the gifts, if ever unearthed, and I could stand before them
their sight would hang my hand midair over my mouth
before I would be brave enough to pick the first one up—
a tiny glass bottle filled with oil, that when dropped
one drop at a time, could turn the insignificant into significant,
change the blank inside of a matchbook
into the most sacred diary, and a dirty penny
into a tool to count the dead.

If I did dream the name of a town that could save my life
then the next morning I'd wake high on adrenaline,
run to the drawer in the kitchen where the maps are kept—
and stand stiff in front of the atlas when I realized
the name of the town I dreamt was before me in the index.

Afraid of a dream that seemed more like a prophecy,
I'd lower myself slowly, inch by inch, down
onto the couch covered in dog hair, and sit there stunned
until the cigarette in my hand burned to my knuckles.

Only then would I rise to pack a small bag of belongings, snap
the light shut in the living room and rush my dog, Rorschach
out of the house and into the truck. I would tell no one
where I was going in case it proved a bust, only leaving a short
note on the kitchen table for my girlfriend that said,

Dear Lamby,

Last night I dreamt of a place where sadness could be ripped in half, and sickness, tied idly in knots all day. There were signs everywhere that said, Camus, Idaho. When I woke up I wanted to see if Camus was a real town so I looked it up in the atlas and there it was. I know this sounds crazy, but I have to go and find out if there's anything there that can help me make sense of this world.

xoxox

P.S. I took Rorschach.

It's not just that I dreamt the name of a place

that housed books filled with lost equations
to explain the mundane and the heinous,
but it was the actual way I flew through space
that urged me to believe in the town I went to that night.

It wasn't the normal kind of dream flying
where, in the middle of panic and heart-pounding retreat,
I remember I can fly, and get a running start and do it—
no, I flew too fast to be alive, awake or dreaming,
and I was scared I'd been taken, angel hands under each
of my arms, and lifted off somewhere I never believed in.

If it was true that I died that night when I fell asleep
then death felt good, like I was in a city
where no one walked or took the subway.
Instead we all took armstrokes the lengths of our bodies
and pushed the velvet edges of water down
from our heads to our hips. We were all dead, swimming
underwater, euphoric and silent in an afterlife public city pool.

While I swam through space, me and everyone around me
moved with the undeniable giddiness of being high or about to
        come.
It was that feeling of how your body gets abducted inch by inch
nerve by nerve, until finally after burning and want
and want— the white sheet gets thrown over your brain,
like it's a chair in a mansion, during the months no one's there.

Regardless, it was the good kind of dead—like if a lucky few
stumbled upon a cave in the middle of their rainy, jobless city,
but not just the luck of finding the cave, but the word
that doesn't exist for what goes beyond luck,
when around one wet and dripping cave corner
their feet stop short, and they see a blue-green pool
cupped in cave-hands, and held out to them.

Dear Lamby,

Saw this cute diner so I pulled over for a bite to eat. Inside, I had this feeling I was being watched. When I turned my head I saw these truckers glaring at me.

"Ever heard of a town in Idaho called Camus?" I asked the waitress.

"I've never been to Idaho," she said.

I glanced over my shoulder one last time, then left a big tip and drove off before the truckers could get me.

xoxox

The next night, the chest-high bricks of a well
sat across a field from me, I walked over, looked down
and dropped parts of myself, knowing I would drink
them again someday—what I'm saying is,
I wrapped myself in maple leaves, tossed myself
toward cleaner water and broke my own surface.

It's not always like this, the dreams—strange and poetic
holy and calm. Last night it was a bar where sleazy men pushed
hundred-dollar bills down my dress—everyone laughed,
let's leave, I kept saying,

but my girlfriend wanted to stay,
so in my frustration, I broke a pint glass
on the bar and swung the jagged edge at my wrist,
the blood paused a moment before it spilled out the white gash,
and like always, before I swing a broken glass at my arm,

there's a moment where I hesitate,
not really wanting to.

So you can understand a little better,
how a disgruntled waitress might pack her dog
and few belongings and head for a town
she dreamed the name of, searching for something to break
the spell of monotonous, morbid night speak.

Dear Lamby,

I had to pull over because I was crying so hard. Rorschach licked my hand like an animal mother nurses her wounded young. I was sobbing, "I'm crazy, I'm crazy, Oh my God, Rorschach, I'm crazy." All of a sudden, TAP, TAP, TAP. This state trooper is hitting his nightstick on the glass and saying, "Ma'am is everything okay in there?" What was I supposed to say, "Oh, it's just that things have been a little hard with my girlfriend lately, and now I'm headed for Idaho because I read too much into a dream I had"?

"Can you hear me, Ma'am?"

I hadn't said anything and was staring blankly out the window.

"Secure the Dalmatian, and step out of the car," the state trooper said.

Rorschach went bonkers, lunging and growling at the window. I slipped out of the truck sideways and locked her inside.

"Sniff, sniff, I'm sorry officer. I was driving along when I realized it was exactly one year ago to the day that my dog consumed an entire combat boot and almost died when her intestines twisted around it. I'm just so grateful she's alive."

"This dog here?" the state trooper asked.

"Yessir."

"Ma'am, you're going to need to move the vehicle as soon as you've gathered yourself. It's against the law to be parked on the shoulder of the road."

"Even if you're crying, it's against the law?" I asked.

xoxox

Dear Lamby,

Couldn't sleep. Pulled off on a "scenic overpass" and tried to curl up with the seat leaned back, but whenever I began to doze off, a huge truck would whiz or rattle by. My lips are so chapped they feel like two corn chips glued to my face. Besides the "scenic overpass" not being scenic, I feel better than before when I wrote you about the cop. It's weird the way my moods swing. One minute I'm suicidal, the next I'm flashing my tits at truckers for fun. They'd probably get out a shotgun and kill me if they knew I was a dyke. But maybe not, those rest area men's rooms are a regular Sodom and Gomorrah. Now I'm missing you, wishing you were here with me in the rest area lobby, first a Tab Cola from the vending machine, then a make-out scene in the grubby bathroom stall.

xoxox

To trace my nose in that space between her collarbones
to move it endlessly in that tiny groove
the space I always pretend is a thumbprint dent in a piecrust,

to know, that despite the grandfather—the magician
who molested all the girls in the family
who pulled pennies from behind their ears
as he pretended to levitate them
so he could put his hands under their shirts
one at a time, three generations of women,
three generations of silence . . .

to know, despite this—a counteraction exists—
a violet sky like a tablecloth stretched taut overhead
stars like salt spilled across the night

to know for every bad drawer or memory, molded shut
from magician child-molester grandfathers
a counteraction or two, your eyes—two great brown holes—

and what if I'd never seen them—been drawn dumb and giddy—
then how would I have fallen into each of them
like they were elevator shafts in the tallest buildings?

Dear Lamby,

I'm somewhere between Cleveland and Toledo. I decided to sleep in the back of the truck in a rest area because I couldn't find any cheap motels. Every time I'm about to drift off, Rorschach goes into a barking frenzy. Apparently, everyone in the parking lot is the enemy. Well, it's 3 a.m. and the last time I fell asleep, a basketball team pulled in next to me and started a scrimmage right in front of the truck. I thought Rorschach was going to break through the glass and kill them. Finally, they went back to their van. Then two minutes later one kid came back and started to bounce the ball again. Bounce, bark. Bounce, bark. Bounce, bark. I'm so exhausted, I feel like crying. He's still there, dribbling around the truck.

xoxox

Who made this place, kept one piece of parking lot pure
like the facedown side of a shirt in a store window?

Whose idea, the parking lot, a place with nothing there
to interrupt a dream or the song of it that plays in his head,
the song that rung by rung unfolds the ladder beneath him
so he can climb deep down into a place unfaded?

What architect drew the plan, made the others sleepy
put him alone there at 3 a.m., dribbling, bouncing, perfecting?

And the boy, all these years, how'd he do it,
not let anyone steal his hope, keep it safe between
his sock and his ankle?

What town did he come from, what team, unfunded
that on the way to a tournament, they'd sleep in a rest area?

How was it that he'd be the one that did not sing
in the van with the others, but instead, saw the day
he would be lifted onto shoulders and carried
across the court, while confetti rained inside a gymnasium,

and what was the chance, I'd see him slip on the gravel,
fall down stunned   and get up again,
before I realized, I knew his desire:
the one lit window glowing
from within an abandoned warehouse?

Dear Lamby,

I gave up trying to sleep in the rest area around 5 a.m. and got back on the road. After a few hours of searching for somewhere deserted to sleep, I saw a closed DISCOUNT MATTRESS SUPER STORE. I pulled into the empty parking lot, thinking it was ideal since no one would be around for Rorschach to bark at. God, it felt good to sleep, even if it was only a few hours. I can't believe I'm already in Indiana and it's only the second day of my trip. It's like I'm stuck inside a calendar that banks give away. The same white picket fence running beside me, the same billowy cloud hanging like a piñata in the distance.

xoxox

Each curve in the road, each place it disappears
into low fog and pre-dawn light, when you can't see
where it leads, is a front door cracked open
of a life you want to live, but can't live here—

whatever that means, to each of us:
leaving the man or woman who beats us,
finding an adequate hospital to treat our cancer,
running broken-hearted to the other side of the earth,
learning to read.

I want to go places I've never been
because I haven't failed there yet.

I want to journey, like a town flooded, *moved on*
despite that the people and things I love
float, ruined, down the street beside me.

I want to be like the field, burned black, where trees stand
with charred, nubbed branches twitching toward the sky,

how did they do it, travel, one burned tree
by one burned tree to get there, together in that field

did they follow maps, were the trunks
of unburned trees marked with ash to guide the way?

How did they elude us, one by one
creep past the truckers asleep on the roadside,
past the blue-gray metal roof of a decaying shack,

past the mountain that planes straight up from the road
and its soft dirt that tempts us to screw our fingers
into the wet earth, feel it push under our nails and climb up,

how did we not see the burned trees walking
through this place filled with charred bone, lost teeth,
and where were we looking when the woman began

to pick charcoal from the weeds, to draw up her fear
like flames to her breast, like a woman enveloped
in her breaking and her breaking away?

Dear Lamby,

I just heard something moving slowly through the underbrush. I'm curled up in the shell of the truck and Rorschach is plastered to my chest. She keeps trying to wriggle out of my arms, but I won't let her. I went to take a shower in the campground, and I saw this article taped on the bathroom mirror. Two women hikers were found with their wrists bound and their throats slashed in Shenandoah National Park. They were lesbians. As I read it I thought, I remember this story, and then I realized I was thinking about lesbians who were shot execution style in the Appalachian Mountains. These were different murdered lesbian hikers. I ran back to the truck and brought Rorschach into the shower with me. Holding her leash under my foot, I soaped up as fast as I could.

xoxox

The women hikers were murdered for being lesbians.
The sound of that drones in and out,
soon I don't know what happened exactly—
that it's been written about already,
the stories not straight, the pieces no longer whole,
I can't separate one murdered lesbian couple from the next:
what happened, who were they, what happened. . . ?

Just yes or no, did the crickets go on cricketing,
did the violet sky stay violet above it all—
someone slept close while this happened,
what did they dream?

Did anyone hear them struggle, did pieces of their screams
flutter into the air and brush the wing of a bird?
Did these murdered women know it was coming,
not directly, but did their bodies know—
before they knew there was trouble,
did they kiss like in dreams, when you try
to seduce the unattainable stranger
with lies and promises, with everything in them,
did they kiss like that?
How will we know, whether they were good or bad
for each other now, when we can't even keep
this murdered lesbian separate from that?

❖ ❖

Maybe somewhere a honey-colored wheat field
has been set aside, solely as a mourning place
for parents ruined by the death of their child.

These shattered masses could come
following the numb tread of their own footsteps
and tilt their heads that say only
why why   why   toward the sky
until their unmanageable grief flew from their chests
like the most glimmering flock of black birds.

Not a place that rewards blind faith—
not Heaven—or the story of Job—
not the dead child coming back to life,
but a square of shadow on an abandoned wheat field
that when visited—rubbed grief-dulled senses bright again—
gave the mother's mouth back the blood-sweet juice
of a pomegranate, and the father, his favorite
memory of walking through a thick cloud
of jasmine on a particular summer night.

And how the children disappeared—leukemia
or freak accident, suicide or drunk driving, or worse
if they withdrew from the way disagreement
collects over the years and drives one from the other.
I wish there was a place for these broken-hearted parents to go.

Not the same place my father wanted to go when I was fourteen.
He said, *I want to go into the woods and never come out.*
He didn't, but for a while I feared the night
when the house was quiet and the family slept.
He'd load his sleeping bag and shotguns into the truck
and drive off before anybody awoke.
I wish there was a place for broken-hearted fathers to go.
And a place for the daughters who inherit the same traits,
but not the one-room cabin forever in the background of grainy
amateur video Sasquatch sightings, not Hotel Unabomber,
not hermithood.

But a town that when found, found too would be hands
capable of brushing the cobweb of despair
off the face of the ill and bestow the seemingly meaningless
with a long-awaited lifetime award of achievement,

a town where the numb legs of the self-hating and guilty
could tingle and wake, as if from coma—
where the unnoticed rose up and triumphed,
where the smoothest curve of a hip
found its way to the shyest mouth,

where the beautifully worthless, the small and uninteresting,
the broken and water-damaged, the ugly and fearful,
could gather together in private, sign a pact in blood,
and work silently into the night to settle the score.

I wish it was just a matter of knowing where to look—
that it was the indisputable next step after the missing child's
tuft of hair and bloody dress were found,
that the mother's wanting and unwanting feet would be forced
to move forward—that her eyes forced to comb the forest,
and plummet to the bottom of the river.
When the bloated arm rose to the surface,
then the path that that pale finger pointed out
would have to be followed.

Dear Lamby,

According to my map, I drove through Brooklyn, Iowa, and didn't even know it. Maybe it's a sign from God. I'm going to backtrack and check it out.

xoxox

When it was clear which way I needed to walk,
twine would wrap the tragedies I almost didn't survive
before they were loaded, heavy, into a rickety cart
and pushed light-headed toward a town claimed
capable of blotting ink-stains off the hands of misfortune.
Before me were those who'd arrived already—
an enormous snake of women, lined up and, one by one,
handing rapes back to their rapists like broken toys,

and children, on all fours, with their tongues curled
over their bottom lips, folding the corners of poverty
into paper airplanes, and preparing on the count of three
to sail them, millions, into the sky.

Imagine the cruelty of contrast didn't exist:
no mudslide to drown the woman who'd already beat her cancer,
no Trump Taj Mahal built on top of a neighborhood of run-
        down houses,
no family dressed in casino uniforms sitting on their stoop
and staring weary-faced from behind a broken handrail.

What could it feel like to know things were shifting,
to return home and the roaches and mice had gone,
two days, three, then four in a row? The tenement starts
to feel like a home, the fruit is put in a bowl on a table,
and left out the whole day.
And the ripped linoleum turns into a wooden floor—mopped
and gleaming—and a window, anywhere, that if your head
is right, allows your eyes a swimming-pool blue sky
that can't help but drown out the constant calculations:
If I buy the juice, I can't buy the paper towels . . .

A sky that lets you forget for a second the ravaged faces
on your block: a methadone clinic, a homeless shelter,
and a XXX sex shop. Thank God for the sex shop.
Every day on your way to work you look in the door

and smile at the same white inflatable sheep
dangling from the ceiling and turning in the air-conditioned
    breeze.

Imagine *believing*, even after everything
had taught us there was nothing to believe.
An unseen hand pushing on your shoulder blade
until you turned toward the woman or man that you loved
and felt worth as much as the first day of spring
urging its wet sun-warmed head through the shell.

What would it mean for a sky so beautiful to be a mistake?
Not a sky, but a scarf unknowingly dragged through the
    centuries—
not a breathtaking sunset, but the hem of a temp worker's skirt,
shut and forgotten in the bottom of a car door and driven miles,
out of this town and into the next.

What would it mean if this mistake sky, this genetic
mishap was the spark to patch up a life, to strip back
the places that were bubbled and ugly and smooth them,
to let a wrecking ball level the whole thing
like the most condemned of condemned buildings,
so it could be rebuilt?

The unbelievable cruelty of contrast—
the way the desperate gather the last of their money,
wrap it in a scarf, set it all down on a number,
wait for the wheel to stop turning, and look
to where the ball has fallen.

Dear Lamby,

I'm losing hope that there is a place without pain. Went to THE TAP ROOM, one of two bars that I saw in Brooklyn, Iowa. It was over a hundred degrees. I wanted to bring Rorschach in, but the bartender wouldn't let me. So I ordered a Budweiser and she said, "Bottle or can?" I got the bottle and told her I was from Brooklyn, New York.

"Looks like you're a long way from home," she said before walking to the other end of the bar to talk to someone else.

I worried Rorschach's brain was simmering away in the truck. There was a guy sitting at a table in front of me, who barely looked twenty-one, talking to his girlfriend. He was getting a football scholarship or a job offer, and kept clasping his girlfriend's hands, saying, "And they said if in a few months things are still good, then . . ." She didn't look happy. I wondered if he was leaving her behind. He was getting out. You could tell by the way he held her hands with both of his, his arms stretched across the table. I left and went to the grocery store for ice. The econo-size pack of pepperoni in my cooler had been floating in warm water for two days. I was afraid if I waited much longer I'd get food-poisoned. This woman, maybe thirty, who looked fifty, was ahead of me in line. She was buying white bread, chocolate milk and BBQ sauce with her food stamps. She had bruises on her legs and was wearing a bikini top, like she'd been lying out in her backyard. I got my ice and got out of there. I didn't even know it was Friday night. On the radio the DJ kept asking everyone what they were going to do. People called in and said, "Drive around, look for parties, pick up girls."

xoxox

A thousand ways to be lost in this country—
good lost, bad lost—people pushed by broom edges,
flicked by bristle tips into corners . . .

Who plots a way out, what kind of person has it in them
to stand before a mirror, straight-razor in hand,
and cut the rut from their life as if it were a malignant
penny-shaped birthmark on the side of their neck?

After despair came, like a delivery boy to your door
every day for a week, and after you signed the clipboard
and reached for the package, he took your hands
and bent each finger back, until your hands were not hands,
but two sets of broken, crooked twigs . . .

who still has the strength to plan a breakout,
dig a tunnel with a spoon
tap on a cell wall at night, letter by letter
spelling out Rilke poems to encourage their comrades?
Who doesn't get found
is left unplucked from their stagnant life
like a penny in the dirt of a dustpan?

Who, when they find out their husband is having an affair,
can't hack the only plant in their yard to death with a shovel?

Who isn't interesting enough to help—

what forgotten woman sits in her yard in a lawn chair
with a can of soda pressed to her thigh, and the radio
blaring the death toll of Texans
who were victims of a record heat wave?

Whose inner voice sits quiet like an obedient dog
and never says,   *go   go   go.*

Dear Lamby,

Greetings from the Ogallala, Nebraska, Welcome Center. To make a long story short, I've felt like blowing my head off all day. You know when you feel like you can't even make the dog happy. I saw this almost-dry riverbed on the side of the interstate, so I pulled off hoping to let Rorschach run in circles. As soon as I opened the truck door, I was greeted by an eightysomething-husband-and-wife-pamphlet-wielding-welcome-to-Nebraska-team. They started to spew information to convince me to go Lake McConaughy, Nebraska's largest lake and recreation center, which incidentally was only three miles down the road.

"Rorschach can be very unpredictable in crowds," I said, which was true, but also my desire to be around happy-jet-skiing-people was zero.

"Can I let her run around down there?" I asked pointing to the glorified sewer ditch that had looked like a riverbed from the road.

"Well, I don't know if it's safe, there's not really a path," the husband said.

"I won't be long," I promised, "my dog's been stuck in the truck all day."

"Wellll," he hesitated, "Lake McConaughy is so much nicer . . ." His voice continued on behind me as I climbed down through the high grown weeds and cactus, "Ogallala bears little resemblance to the 1874–1884 Ogallala. During that period the town, a cattle-shipping point on the railroad, it was known as the 'Gomorrah of the Plains' . . ."

I'm only 114 years late, I thought as I felt a cactus plant sink its teeth into my calf.

xoxox

P.S. I've been reading tons of Emily Dickinson.

I started Early—Took my Dog—
And Visited the Sea—
Except the Sea—was not a Sea—
But a Half-Evicted—river

My feet Adorned—in socks and boots—
felt Water—wiggle by—

God—pulled the Chain, on anger's Lamp
Sun, cursed from the Sky—

Satanic Sulfur—Bastard Moss—
Mosquitoes, swirled around—

And I, fixed—in calf-high stream
watched, Sorrow's horses, Drown—

From above—Trash was thrown—
A line—Perfected—lay

Drunken Arms—from passing Cars—
Delivered—every Day—

My Dog, ran circles—in the sand—
Her mouth, Clamped—'round a bone—

Unspectacular—she had Found it—
Common, from a Deer—

And I with her—in sewage Ditch
Made our Heaven—Here.

Dear Lamby,

The truck smells like dead deer. Rorschach found a leg bone in the riverbed and spent the entire twelve hours we drove today with her eyes bulging out, tearing the veins and marrow from it. I thought I was going to throw up from the smell, but I didn't have the heart to take it from her and throw it out the window. It was after nine, and on the horizon there was still a strip of white sky left, with the night coming down all around us. I raced toward it, and when I came over the top of a hill, on the other side the white strip got bigger. It was like someone was holding a gap of daylight up, as if it were the bottom of a fence—and if I was quick enough, I'd be able to squeeze through on my stomach, out of this world and into the next. That's how I found myself in Laramie, Wyoming.

xoxox

What could it mean, a night that wouldn't completely fall
but waited, held the door open for you
even though you were all the way across the street?

A strip of diffused light, pulled haphazard across the base
of a horizon, like a small ceramic lamp trying to shine
behind a white sheet, making you want to rush
toward it—hit the gas in your exhaustion,
swerve awkward around each bend of the unlit highway?

What if you started to drive only at night,
found yourself chasing an illuminated space,
the thickness of four stacked phone books
held by an invisible arm, way out there?

If you were drawn to the last pieces of daylight,
the same way you were drawn to certain women
because they were delinquents and hoodlums,
because there were only a few who stood shoulder-
to-shoulder and held the night off as long as they could?

Dear Lamby,

Spent the night in a motel trying to watch the scrambled porn chan-
nel. Only managed to see the occasional breast and hear the plot—a
dominatrix who was being stalked by a psycho trick. It made me
think of all the dykes in San Francisco I knew who were sex work-
ers. This morning I walked Rorschach near the train tracks while
I waited for my oil to be changed. I felt curiously attracted to the
kid who was working on my truck. I wondered what it would be
like to live in a place like this and have a boyfriend who worked at
the filling station. There was a postcard stand in the office and one
had a picture of Laramie, and on the back, the history of the town.
Butch Cassidy was in prison for eighteen months here, and also the
first female jurors served in March 1870. Then it said, this hasn't
happened yet, but in October 1998, two boys will lure a twenty-one-
year-old gay student out of a bar, rob, pistol whip, and tie him to
a fence leaving him for dead. A bicyclist will find him barely alive.
He will never regain consciousness and die a week later. One of his
murderers will say he was embarrassed when the guy flirted with
him in a bar.

xoxox

What would it be like to run through fields at night again,
reckless with dew-wet branches whipping my upper arms,

every branch the mitt of a monster, tentacle
of a killer land-sea octopus, grabbing to take me back?

When did it happen, my extraordinary fears disappeared
and I turned to find myself surrounded. . . ?

Midway through my teens, I woke in a country
knowing what happens to gay people, without knowing any.

He was strung to the fence, barely alive, head bashed in.

Midway through my life, I found myself, book open,
my favorite villains slipping from the pages,

the cardsharp, back pocket stretched
over a flask, each of his girlfriends waiting
in their separate homes for him, these were his sins.

This isn't how I want my criminals motivated:
bigot brain saying, *smash his head, smash his head.*

This isn't how I want the girlfriends of my criminals:
hiding bloody clothes, standing by men like this.

◆   ◆

Five nights in a row, the sun going down, daytime's last breath,
each curve of a hundred-curve leaf sculpts itself black into the
        sky,

the half-lit wavering sun, like the electric company shutting
pieces of power off as unpaid bills pile up,

first the outlet for the toaster, the lamp next to the bed,
but the joke's on them, plenty of times I've loved without light.

Without light, I found you in my living room
next to the coat rack, back against the wall,
the hours dying slow around us, like poisoned mice,

my hands held your face, and your face held your eyes,
and your eyes: small yellow-green places far away—
the light of a lamp on a desk
where someone sits desperately trying to decide something . . .

I wish I'd told you that night what I'd been wanting to for weeks
and I wish I'd told you what never occurred to me until now.

A thousand ways to fall in love
with a married woman in this country.

I did it while working at a restaurant.

Found myself collecting things to give her when she was single:

One. The losing racetrack ticket that had been on my kitchen
    table for a month.

Two. A line from a Nabokov story, mother sifting through
pictures of her son before his full-fledged mental illness:
*Age six—that was when he drew wonderful birds with human
    hands and feet,
and suffered from insomnia like a grown-up man.*

Three. A star-shaped middle of what anise grows on
that I found on the stainless steel kitchen counter where I work.

Four. The reason why I picked the anise star up,
part flower, part starfish, part prehistoric spider,
driven to reach my hand out to wherever you were that day.

Five. The thousand places I can think of us together,
today at three-thirty and fifty-five degrees,
some spring slipped past the winter warden,

and I wanted to be driving, windows down, music blaring,
and have a place on your neck that I've never seen,
turned toward the blurred buildings, the ugly shrubs,
the paint-chipped lampposts, your neck catching the light
of that bright winter afternoon.

Six. My hands flat on your belly, as if that smooth skin
was the glass side of an aquarium, and you could know

giant neon fish, I stood before them once the same way,
the tips of my sweaty fingers against the cold glass
wishing I could be in the tank without killing them.

The deep wish not to destroy wore the costume of a bird,
flew and flapped inside me, I felt it frenetic,
beat the sides and insides of me.

I wanted to heave my body against the door of time
against my own talent to ruin and devote
my life to nervously, wondrously, touching you.

Seven. This sentence:
Beginnings, endings, that's it whether we like it or not,
no one remembers the fiftieth time they fucked their lover,
unless it was the time she shoved six needles through my chest,
or the time I saw the bite mark bruise,
not my own, on her thigh.
Tell me the truth, how long until I find myself
throwing the dog's full bowl of water across the kitchen again,
because you moved on with your life and I stayed heavy-footed
in the linoleum, stupid, trying to resuscitate the broken mop.

After a month, would we want to back
unnoticed from each other into a crowd?

You think I fall in love all the time.

I should tell you the truth about something.
This week I asked three people to marry me.
You, my ex-girlfriend, and the librarian.

I know you're wondering why the librarian.

She found the book I'd been looking for forever.

When she emerged from a back room with the book,
I cried, *You're the big hero!*
She blushed and waved her hands nervously in front of her,
no, no, she said and again I cried, *my hero, my hero*—
her shy hands resumed knitting an invisible sweater above her
     belly . . .
what she said next is why I wanted to marry her:

*If you went to library school you would've known how to find the
     book too.*

So how long do you think it would last with us, if from there
I saw myself licking the librarian's sweaty back in my bed
and giggling, *You're the big hero, you're the big hero*
as I fed her Gin Sling after Gin Sling
and had her tell me why she wanted to be a librarian?

I don't even know if she has a husband
because her hands were so balled up I couldn't see her ring
     finger.
What if I told you I wouldn't want to have an affair with her
unless she slurred and spilled her drink on the edge of my filthy
     bed,
or if it ever happened, that I licked the librarian's salty back,
I'd still call you afterwards the same night,
tell you to meet me for a drink somewhere,
in some smoky, lonely palace?

Dear Lamby,

I'm in Idaho drinking my last warm beer. As soon as I crossed the Utah/Idaho border I went to the Information Center. The old man working there looked exactly like the old man at the Ogallala, Nebraska Welcome Center. I'm starting to wonder if these senior volunteers aren't holograms. From the window, I could see Rorschach tied to a picnic table waiting for me. I asked the hologram what was the best interstate to get to Camus. He said, "Camus?"

I said, "Yes sir, Camus, Idaho."

"You mean, Camas," he said.

"No sir, Camus, like the writer, Albert Camus."

"There's no Camus in Idaho, Ma'am."

My heart began the slow tumble of a flowerpot off a fire escape.

"It's right here on my map," I said, sliding my finger down to "C" where Camus should have been.

It said Camas County. Lamby, there's no Camus.

xoxox

PETER

For beauty is nothing but the beginning of terror,
which we still are just able to endure,
and we are so awed because it serenely disdains
    to annihilate us.
Every angel is terrifying.

—Rainer Maria Rilke, from "The First Elegy"

This morning I started out for Camas, my last stab at finding a miracle town somewhere. It was so hot, Rorschach didn't have the energy to bend down and drink from her bowl. After an hour of driving, we came upon this huge hand-painted billboard that said CAVE in crude, brown, letters. I'd always wanted to go to a cave, so I followed a series of arrows down a gravel path, until I saw a tiny wooden shack that said, CAVE OFFICE. Leaving Rorschach in the truck, I went in. A young boy emerged from behind the desk, with a book in his hand. At first I thought he was a girl because he had an androgynous Dutch-Boy haircut.

"Hi," I said.

"Hi."

On the wall behind him was a sign that said, ADULTS $4.00.

"Is the cave open?" I asked.

"Yeah."

"Can I bring my dog in?"

"Yeah."

The room felt like no one had been in it for years. He must sit here all day reading books, I thought. I got Rorschach out of the truck and went back inside the CAVE OFFICE. When I reentered the room, the boy emerged exactly as he had just moments before, with his blond-brown hair in his face, and the book folded in half over his hand. He looked at me like I was someone different than the person who was just there thirty seconds ago. Weakly, he smiled.

"Is the cave far from here?" I asked.

He shook his head no, and pointed toward the back of the office. The office was also a MUSEUM filled with dusty, taxidermied animals, birds in glass cases, long bones in trays all around the floor, and cheap rings made out of railroad nails in a giant candy jar on the counter. I paid him the four dollars and started toward the back of the museum where he'd signaled the cave was. Rorschach was choking herself, trying to lunge at the prehistoric bones and glass cases filled with stuffed hawks. I tugged at her leash, trying to keep her from knocking over a stuffed hawk.

"You need a lantern," the cave boy shouted after me.

My heart cemented shut inside me. Turning toward him I said, "I need a lantern?"

"Yeah."

"Is it scary in the cave?" I asked.

"Some people find it scary."

"Are there animals down there? Will I need to wear something besides these flip-flops?"

"No," he said.

"No, meaning there aren't animals, or no I won't need different shoes?" I wanted to get the animal thing straight right now.

"There aren't animals," he said.

"If I'm not back in fifteen minutes, come get me," I pleaded.

"It takes longer than fifteen minutes," he said.

What had possessed me to come here? When I saw the CAVE billboard and enthusiastically sped down the gravel road, I imagined a freshly painted handrail, well-lit stalactites, and if not a tour guide then at least other tourists. In spite of everything, I wound down the gravel path until the opening of the cave came into sight. I wished I had worn different shoes now. Pebbles were getting caught between the flip-flop bottom and my foot. Rorschach, eager to meet our respective deaths, tugged toward the cave. I was off-balanced, with the lantern in one hand and a Dalmatian at full-tilt in the other—the whole time pebbles stabbed into the bottom of my feet. We entered the cave. Immediately I wanted to cry, turn around, and beg the boy at the desk to come with me. There was enough light from the opening to see burned-out lightbulbs hanging in irregular distances along the path. After three steps it would be pitch black. I continued to take steps toward the center of the cave. The lantern was a joke. The only thing it allowed me to see was an enormous shadow of my clenched jaw bobbing against the rock wall. The burned-out lightbulbs were adding up. Where were the ice sculptures and ponds of blue-green water? What if this whole cave thing was a facade to rob tourists? I'd be the famous statistic of the robbery victim who was killed for not carrying any money. My mom always told me to keep twenty dollars in my sock so in case I was robbed, I'd have something to give the robber. I could see the headline now, killed for fifteen cents! The taxidermied birds in glass cases back at the museum flashed in my brain. I pictured my face on the stuffed hawk. I began to race down the trail, my flip-flops slapping the floor. Somehow, the sentence being repeated inside me was, "You paid the four dollars, you can't turn around." Ror-

schach would protect me if someone jumped out. Giant shadows surrounded me. The occasional drip, dripped. I came upon the first informative sign—a list of minerals the cave was made of. Holding the lantern up to the wall, I tried to see a mineral. A B-movie I'd seen in the seventh grade called Tourist Trap *flashed in my brain. It was about a man who kidnapped women and covered them in plaster, leaving only their nose open so they could breathe. Then before he'd cover their nostrils, he'd say, "Good-bye baaaaby!" He was turning them into mannequins, but I can't remember why. I mean, besides the fact that he was crazy. We began to run—passing another burned-out lightbulb, an extension cord, more dripping. The shadows circled like sharks. I kept telling myself, I'm not cool enough to die this way. Another sign—about volcanoes and how they relate to caves. Slap, slap, slap. Rorschach was busy smelling the blood droplets of similar past fools that were embedded in the floor. The third sign talked about harmless bats with such and such wingspan. BATS! But the boy at the desk had promised no animals. Were bats a technical exception, like reptile or bird family? I envisioned bumping into the bat nest, and the bats swarming toward my face—Mama Bat in the background with her index finger pointed at me, shaking it back and forth and going, tisk, tisk, tisk. "Bats are good," the sign said, "they eat insects." What's wrong with insects being in a cave? It wasn't a restaurant. There was no way I could deal with a bat flying into my face. With the last of my energy, I slapped my way to the final sign. YOU HAVE REACHED THE END OF THE TRAIL, GO NO FURTHER! YOU CAN NOW SEE WHY CAVES WERE GREAT PLACES FOR BEARS, SLAVES ON THE RUN, MOONSHINERS AND MURDERERS! It never occurred to me that I would have to go back the way I came, even though that's what distinguishes a cave from a tunnel. I looked for a lost decanter of moonshine. With the fear of bears, bats, rapists, and murderers on my trail, I started back to the cave opening. In my brain was the villain's voice from* Tourist Trap *saying, "Good-bye baaaaby." Abruptly Rorschach stopped. I covered my nose waiting for some stubble-chinned man to jump out and slap plaster over my nostrils. Rorschach hunched over and began taking a dump. Baffled at my desire to respect a place that had caused me such suffering, I picked up after her when she was finished. Bag of shit* and careening Dalmatian in one hand and lantern in the other, I raced down the trail, until the light of the entrance became a larger and larger pinhole. A flock of winged silhouettes erupted out of the belly of light. "Why me, why me?" I cried dropping my head and making a final lunge toward outside, just long enough to see the sparrows I thought were BATS fly out the mouth of the cave and into the afternoon.

Exhausted, I headed up the gravel path, back to the CAVE OF-FICE. I felt strangely close to the boy who made this experience possible for me. I wanted to ask him what people found attractive about being in the cave. Rorschach and I entered the back of the museum, and I choked up on the leash so she couldn't get too much of a lead. She wasn't budging though. The cave office cat was glaring at her. I was not in the mood for cat/dog trivial bullshit, and I dragged her to the front. The boy emerged.

Putting my lantern down, I said, "I've never felt so scared in my life."

He smiled. He smiled a lot. The cat lunged at Rorschach and she cowered. I wanted to know this boy inside and out. He stood in front of me with his Dutch-Boy haircut and book in one hand. He looked busy. There was a population of four people in his town, and no one else was visiting this backyard cave, what could he have to do? He seemed restless to get back to his book.

"Do you go in the cave every day?" I asked.

"Yeah."

"What do you do, read?" I asked.

"Just mess around."

I hope he doesn't jerk off down there, I thought. I simply wanted him to be the shy-intellectual-paintboy-haircut-reading-cavedweller whom I was going to run away with. His thumb tapped the spine of the book. I felt pressured to say the right thing so he would rather talk to me than go back to his book. What was he reading? He looked about fifteen. He must live in the other wood shack next to the cave office with his family. I wonder where the family was. I didn't even want to go to Camas anymore. I wanted to stay with him, run through the desert at night—explore the cave with him as my guide, holding his sweaty pink hand in mine, take him away from his horrible family who kept him from everyone, just so he'd

51

mind the cave. We'd go to Boise, slip into a gay bar, he'd point out the kinds of guys he liked to me, I'd teach him how to kiss . . . "Like this," I'd say, moving my tongue over his, like a basting brush over an uncooked loaf of bread. The roof came crashing in on my fantasy. I'm gay. He's fifteen. At the very least that's abduction. Rorschach lurched away from the cave office cat again. The opportunity for us to bond was slipping away. He hung out in the cave every day. He had to be totally cool or totally crazy. I tried to think of something to say that would make him want to go on a trip with me.

"There was this woman anthropologist or archaeologist or something who was writing a book, I don't remember where, I think Australia, anyway, she went into a cave and lived there for over a year all by herself. She brought all her supplies in and lived without a watch so she had no way to tell whether it was day or night. That whole time she never came out. When she finished her experiment and went back to her life, she killed herself because her reality was so fucked up. She'd lost all sense of time."

He lifted his eyebrows, seeming momentarily interested, and said, "Really?"

"Isn't that intense?"

"Yeah."

Rorschach whined. The cat was moving in on her. I was still holding the bag of shit from the cave. There was so much I wanted to talk to him about, but Rorschach was trying to squirm away from the cat. He'd seemed intrigued when I was telling him the cave story but then began to tap on his book again.

"Well, see you later," I said.

"O.K."

"What's your name?"

"Peter."

"See you, Peter."

"O.K."

I got in the truck, resenting Rorschach and the cave office cat dispute. If she hadn't been there, maybe I could've sat with Peter forever.

JACKPOT, NEVADA

And though I don't know much about madness,
I know it lives in the thin body like a harp
Behind the rib cage. It makes it painful to move.
And when you kneel in madness your knees are glass,
And so you must stand up again with great care.

—Larry Levis, "For Zbigniew Herbert, Summer,
   1971 Los Angeles"

I want night to fall, not the sun going down
but for all that star-bitten black to push into me

fell in love with a boy once, in Idaho
it was his face, the way the blond hair swept across it

sometimes that happens, you look into a face and forget
the fact that the miracle that was supposed to happen, never did

sometimes the moon's enough
and sometimes it isn't

I've overlooked full moons before,
left them thumbtacked,
glowing holy and white in the perfect sky

I left the cave wanting solely to be with Peter. The farther I went, the stronger my urge to go back for him. On the roadside, prisoners picked up trash. I hoped they'd all committed triple murders to be out in that heat. Finally, I reached a sign that said, ENTERING CAMAS COUNTY. *I held my breath, waiting for some sort of feeling to come over me, but none did. I thought I might be directed in some way, the wind changing, a terrible storm, the prophetic face of a cow turning toward me. But the hologram at the Information Center hadn't lied—there was nothing in Camas. No houses. No people. Only sectioned-off ranches. On the border when you leave the county, there's a convenience store and gas station. I pulled in the parking lot, thought about getting gas but didn't. Peter kept running around in my brain. Thought about getting a beer for the truck, but didn't.*

The whole open road and nowhere to go

I held a gun once, loved my hands that kept
the metal smell of the barrel even hours later

loved the breaking wave my stomach became each time I held it

I was pretty sure it wasn't loaded, so I put it to my head

met a guy at an A.A. meeting
who shot himself in the head and lived
he held a job afterwards and everything

knew another guy who got shot
walking to the restaurant where we worked
said it felt like someone threw a rock at the back of his neck

hated guns until I felt one in my hand
the little spy gun, the little Colt .25

the whole open road and nowhere to go

Dear Lamby,

I'm at the Covered Wagon Motel right over the Idaho/Nevada border in Jackpot, Nevada. The marquee out front says, Certainty is a prison. Rooms $19.99 a night. I've been here three days and for three days it's been 105 degrees. I thought I'd win me some money at the roulette wheel. On the contrary, I've lost almost everything and tomorrow I have to check out by eleven. The motel woman shoots me the dirtiest looks, like it's my fault my clothes are filthy. She's a face-painted whore anyway, and if there was a Bible in the nightstand, I'd find the passage that says bad things about women like her, but her motel doesn't have a Bible or a phone. I've been spending my time drinking warm Budweiser and watching COURT TV. Then at five o'clock, I walk across the street and get the $3.99 Prime Rib Dinner. It's big enough so I don't need to eat anything but that for the day. I'm going to really try not to go back to the casino tonight.

xoxox

I don't know much about leaving town
just that the wooden handle that pumps that well
keeps going up and down inside of me.

Once I heard a ship outlined by tiny yellow lights
call out to me through the midnight fog

the ground broke inside me

once my life was a broken bicycle I couldn't get to roll again

and I fell in love with a boy in Idaho
it was the way his blond hair swept across his face

Dear Lamby,

I've got to get out of here before the motel lady kills me. Last night I stacked the chairs up against the door, so if she tried to get in, it would be harder. Rorschach hates being cooped up in the room all day. I don't know what to do next. I thought about calling this guy Peter who I met at a cave, but I don't know if his family would mind if I stayed there. The other option is I could go to Las Vegas. It's only six hours from where I am. But I'd like to feel a little more together before I see my family.

xoxox

An escape route can be anything

one night in Brooklyn, coming home from work,
I kept going, followed the Belt Parkway alongside the water

the shape of ships sat still under the bridge
you couldn't see the ships, just tiny lights all around them

like boat-shaped escape doors, sitting on top of the water
square black holes and rectangles, all lit up

I wanted to yell out to someone sleeping on the ship
ask them to open the escape door for me

I almost fell asleep that night driving
my arms tingled, tired from holding the steering wheel

the next day I looked around my house
not sure if I'd come back and drove to ATLANTIC CITY

walking across the boardwalk—the bottom half of my pants
were wet from waves I didn't move away from—

a drunk man screamed at me and above him
the sun was bright pink and round with the top blown off
pink brains blown across the sky
police dogs growled in a police car,
a woman sang, *Lord, come by here*

I stood numb before his screaming
too sad to move, I stared at the pink, pink sun

I'd been like him before, a fish caught in its own net
glittering gills trying to open against the air

except I was like that for days that turned into years
not years that turned into a life, or an entire family tree.

Dear Lamby,

I tried to call Peter. The woman who answered the phone said Peter was in the cave. She sounded mistrustful. I think it was his mother. I'm afraid to call back in case she has the cops trace the call, even though it's not like I did anything illegal. Unless of course, making new friends is illegal all of a sudden. I'm sorry I've been a bad girl-friend. I took off on this trip to try and figure out how to not be such an infidel. But of course it all turned to shit.

xoxox

Dear Peter,

I hope you get this letter. I'm the woman who came to the cave with my Dalmatian a few days ago. Remember, I told you the story about the archaeologist who killed herself?

Dear Peter,

I'm writing because I'm in a little bit of trouble, and I had a good feeling about you as a person. I think because I've always felt comfortable around people who befriend literature.

Peter,

I'm the woman who came to the cave. Remember, I had the Dalmatian. I thought maybe you'd like to go to THE WRONG NUMBER. *It's a gay bar in Boise.*

Dear Peter,

Is the cave hiring right now?

Dear Peter,

I was there a few days ago with my Dalmatian, and I was wondering if there were currently any career openings at the cave. I know I seemed afraid of the cave, but I could do various odds and ends in the office, and if absolutely necessary, I would go into the cave. I need cash.

Dear Peter,

I made your acquaintance a few days ago. Unfortunately, I didn't have any business cards on me when I visited your cave. In retrospect, I think you might be the perfect candidate for a program my non-profit company puts on called "Big City, for Big Boys." We work at giving small-town kids a shot at seeing the big city.

YEARS LATER,

MONTROSE, PENNSYLVANIA

This is the Hour of Lead—
Remembered, if outlived,
As Freezing persons, recollect the Snow—
First—Chill—then Stupor—then the letting go—

—Emily Dickinson, #341

You learn a lot by watching someone die.
You learn that you are more afraid than them.

The person I saw die, died slow over three days.
We watched her die on Monday.
We watched her die on Tuesday.
We watched her die on Wednesday.
For fourteen hours a day, we watched her die.

People who are dying, know it.
They say things like, *Georgiana, I'm coming home,*
but Georgiana is someone they haven't seen in thirty years.

The doctor said, *there's been some brain damage.*
Her hands swum a backward breaststroke
as she tried to move the heavy sheets off her.

She went from being coherent to incoherent in a matter of
    hours.
We sat around her like inept, moss-covered statues.
We moved with the swift-guilty motions
of the living around the almost-dead,
our big, living smiles fluttered off our faces
and landed like one-colored butterflies on the hospital walls.

At the end she breathed only eight times a minute.
We stood around her in a half-circle and waited for those
    breaths.

When she did breathe— it was like someone who comes up
from being underwater, gasping.
The doctor said, *her breathing will slow down
until it stops completely.*
Every time we thought she'd stopped breathing,
her shut mouth sprang open
like a cuckoo-clock door,
one fat huff
but no wood-painted birds.

The doctor lifted a plastic bag hooked to her catheter
and held it toward us. *Her kidneys aren't working at all,*
he said, showing us the empty bag.

Assorted nurses changed the bedding four times a day
because the toxins oozed out her bloated thighs and elbows.
When I held her hand, it smelled like death.
When I held her hand, I held it for an hour.
I leaned over and kissed her forehead,
without letting go of her hand.

Four times I washed my hand,
four times it smelled like death.

*The fluids will fill her lungs and
she'll be unable to breathe.*

I imagined the leak in my kitchen ceiling,
drop by drop filling the green bucket

and the lives of the nurses that worked
in this ten-patient, two-doctor country hospital.

When watching her die became too much
I'd walk out to the waiting room
and alternate between a 5,000-piece jigsaw puzzle and Psalms.

A nurse dropped her earring
then crawled around and looked for it.
The earring wasn't the only lost object,
days later, I realized the puzzle only had 4,973 pieces.
A floral garden missing part of the rabbit's face and fountain
    base.

Peter, this is how time is marked in hospitals:
the various family members gather around the bed
where the sick family member is dying

they sit quietly for the most part of the day,
although sometimes the uncle reads political
excerpts from the local newspaper

as for the room:
a drab curtain half-pulled around the metal-frame bed
plastic-wood-paneled TV set hanging from the ceiling
and the same pastel-painted sailboat on the wall of every room.

The sheets remained perfectly tucked and unwrinkled
because she was too weak to roll onto the bed's edges,
staying exactly in the middle,
and the fluids leaked out her elbows and thighs,
leaving yellow-pink stains around her like odd-shaped buttons.

My mother sat beside her and embroidered
until she stopped breathing.

Hours after she died, my father broke
out the vacuum cleaner
and started to suck dust off every knickknack
in her decaying house
saying, *Jesus Christ, Jesus Christ*
look at the dust on these things.

I want my family,
my family that I feel ashamed around.
The one that looks like a boy
when the other women
look like women in books or magazines.

I want my family
and I want to walk away from the riddle that is my family.

I want the trees' strength to survive the cold
and the snow-covered rusted tools and branches.

My father kept vacuuming

furious at each layer of dust,
my uncle collected boxes for the Harlequin novels
that filled the back bedroom,
and my mother looked in the phone book
to try and find a place to buy my grandmother
an outfit in which to be buried.
I retrieved objects consecutively,
in the order my father called them out to be dusted.

This is the first time anyone's died on me in a while,
but people used to die all the time,
and I used their funerals as the chance to heave my body
against some woman and sob into her mothball breasts.

Once, six months after a funeral, I was still sobbing—
a radiance entered my room, *went through me*
long enough for one layer of grief to float away.

I didn't give up on you,
I was afraid if I stayed I'd ruin your life.

I packed my bags, made breakfast,
then ran miles through overgrown fields,

to the broken tree where one green apple remained
frozen to a branch

I wanted it to sum up my life

(Was there ever a branch that leaned toward you and
    said   live?)

Do you think it's true
that it happens early,
whether we want to be here or not?

There's a block of wood burning as I write this—
into black squares, that look like windows,
a burning orange block, a hotel with no survivors

how is it I'm petrified to die and petrified to live?

Rorschach curls closer to be near the fire,
I look at the way her ear falls
over the arm of the chair.

Yesterday, sunlight fell on the straight planks
of the porch and everything made sense:

I began to believe in afternoon love affairs again,
if I was inside her—if we were in that cold bedroom,
that cobwebbed attic—under the blanket
that smelled like detergent and winter

after the tears ended—the country road curved
and the trees stood in the night like devoted artists,
my mouth moved around each of her fingers

distracted, she drove past the driveway
where we should have turned.

The facts lie inside my head like old
black-and-white photographs, where nothing happens—
except old women row a boat in an unexceptional pond
while wearing their Sunday hats.
I know she wondered why I bought those violet hats
with ivory bands the other day,

I know I should've bought groceries.
I know I should have paid the telephone bill.

Six months after my grandmother died
I moved into her dilapidated farmhouse with Rorschach,
and a man with yellow boring eyes moved into my brain
he brought his confessions:

murders, accidents
skinny women fell from haylofts.

The house that always sat there was gone
no trace of it, enough markers to prove that this was my life
a rusted rake leaning against the green trash barrel
and in a potted plant, my new lover's lipstick mark
on a crushed out cigarette,

schools of fish swam into the sides of my legs
it was winter, the fish were swimming into my bare legs,
I was afraid.

Dear Peter,

I hope you get this letter, you can't trust the guards here. We are supposed to call them correctional officers. Strange, since we're always being guarded. I'm not supposed to be in contact with you, but this is my official letter of apology. They'll probably give you a page with a bunch of holes in it and only leave the words, "I'm sorry." You looked super-scared when I drove through the front window at the Dairy Queen. The last thing I saw was all that blond hair. You were standing next to the pay phone where I told you to meet me, holding your small red duffel bag. That's the last thing I remember, then I woke up handcuffed to the hospital bed, all bandaged up. My head was killing me, and I felt a terrible sadness. Every time I turned, I heard the sound of broken deer legs dragged through the rocky terrain behind my ribcage. The Dairy Queen was closed. The floor was covered with the yellow plastic signs they put down when they mop so when someone one slips and hurts themselves they can't get away with a lawsuit. I want to call my family, but I don't know how to begin explaining. Can you read this? The pencil isn't writing so well on this brown bag. The bag is from our lunch today. We got two tiny oranges, two pieces of brown bread, and then in a separate plastic bag, two slices of pimento loaf. I guess that's the only way you get people to eat pimento loaf, give it to them while they're in jail. When I said, "We're gonna blow this popsicle stand," I meant it. And no matter what the cops said, I didn't tell you to meet me so I could run you over. It was like this group of invisible thugs held me around the throat and stepped on the gas, and there was this big fat light beam going through my brain, and I felt like I was waking up from an operation, on those kinds of drugs and then everything was black. I would never hurt anybody, but you don't know that. Follow the arrows on the bottom corner to know which bag to go to next. At the cave you changed my life, the way strangers can. The way meeting someone new makes you forget you want to die. Even though I'm a lesbian, I had feelings for you. Even though you were fifteen, or that's how old I guessed you were. "It's lucky for you, he's older," the cops said. Peter, once I was unemployed and I was walking my dog in the park and I saw a slaughtered pig on the rocks in the woods. There was blood everywhere. My heart pounded. When

I looked back, the pig was gone. I want someone to hold me when my skin becomes a shell that's too big for me and I live way down inside it and the voices of people around me are far away like at a campsite across the campground and I'm a penny at the bottom of an elevator shaft. I finished high school. I kept a job for more than five years. Both my parents worked and did not become divorced. People think when you end up on the front of the newspaper, you came from a broken home. I think life is like a giant poker game. You have the possibility to feel great or horrible every few seconds. After the first time I went to jail, I was angry for months afterwards. Whenever I walked—I pretended the police were beating me and I didn't fight back. I took it and never acted hurt. Sometimes I see my dreams sit in a chair, like a nice father, but the chair has armrests made out of hot coils from a stove and there is no way to climb onto the chair and hug the father without getting burned. I'm not a fucked-up person who hurts animals because they can't feel sadness. Some people think it's fun to shoot lizards with a BB gun. I got shot with an air rifle once. My brother pumped the air rifle up to ten and shot me with a mushroom pellet. I miss my brother, Peter. We live such different lives now.

Peter, they've even ruined jail.

Snow falling through the day in chunks the size of round
    crackers.
They've taken the bars off
and replaced them with small unbreakable glass
that even if broken wouldn't be a big enough space
to stick your head out of and feel that snow fall
in giant pieces on your giant cheeks.

Through the cell window yellow light falls
on a boring concrete slab,
the peach stucco walls of the next building
are no place to dream of running.
No smoking, no train in the background.
There's no place left to dream of going.

I wanted to break free, but I wanted to do it with you.
I know you know that kind of desert heat.
Alone with Rorschach we wandered roads
I have the sense to stay away from when pain hasn't pushed me
like the door predictably pushes the cheap rug
each time it opens.
I wanted to be brave together
play a game of checkers with our backs
turned to the firing squad—

the firing squad we could never know.
I wanted to become immune to the plane crashes
that show up every night on the news.
The aftermath: pieces of plane
floating in a small area of our giant ocean.
I watch for hours until they draw out a shoe or heavy passenger.

The shoes of the dead are not that different from the shoes of the
    living.
The black water is lit up by the squid fishermen's lights,
who've come in the middle of the night,

to help find pieces of plane, people,
or to retrieve one lost ring for a mourning family member.

    The plane crashed.
    Everyone died.
    In a few months it will happen again.

Every time I see a plane crash on the news I feel selfish,
as if somehow it were possible to do nothing for months
but set aside grief and the belief in heaven,
like loose branches in a metal pail, beside a wood-burning stove.

I was the stone falling through the water to the bottom
of the pond. I was heavy, cold and tumbling, and no one knew—

Rorschach ran happily in circles in the field
the sun was setting, so the sky was how it is
just before it starts to be night, the late afternoon blue
there was one pinprick star, I swear
and the trees with no leaves
looked black against the almost-dusk

everyone knows the scrawny look
the always-reaching branches
tiny jagged veins, searching to feed something,
nothing there, but the sky's one star.

Thirty trees haloed by the way the last bit of sunlight fell

they stood like a choir

my ears burned from winter
and I did not dive toward that one pinprick hole

scattered shoes and clothing are fished out
and put into plastic bags,
I look to see if I recognize
the wet shoe or sweater pulled
dripping from the water.

I was not living as a soap opera writer for the Hungarian radio
afraid of censors and the government. I was standing in a field
holding a plastic cup half-filled with cranberry juice
because for months I'd felt a pain under my ribs.
Rorschach ran and the sun began to disappear

an airplane trailed white smoke below the pinprick star

I saw a scar being made and soon it would be night
and like all gorgeous scars, it would slip under some sheet
its raised edges given equal chance of being touched or missed.

In the wall there is a woman.
The wallpaper is stained from leaking rain.

Daydreaming was my first addiction.
I used to pretend to be asleep after I woke up
and wish some woman was near me,
that I had my arms around some woman.

I move sluggishly.
My voice has moved ahead of me
and I can't catch up to those words:

promise me nothing, put your mouth on me
spear the first star out of the sky with a stick
and then the first star again and the first star after that
until we're out of breath, and the next day
muscles we didn't even know we had, ache.

My nights are spent interviewing for waitress jobs I don't want
afterwards I go to the only gay bar in a 200-mile radius
winter means an early darkness outside and inside—
in the bar everyone is drunk

twelve-shots-of-cheap-tequila-drunk
I drive home drunk with one hand down my pants
hoping to get arrested, so I could beg the cop to fuck me.

My days are spent reading up on saints:
To become a saint, you need to perform three miracles
before trustworthy witnesses.
(You can't sleep with other people's girlfriends either.)

I woke at six-thirty
to the sound of train wheels
riding over my hands
made a list of things to do
and left it on the kitchen table . . .

THINGS TO DO TODAY TO BE CONSIDERED FOR SAINTHOOD:

1. Mop floor
2. Arrange lightbulb boxes with flush corners
3. Scrub hood above stove

I find myself wanting to be fifteen again
to crawl back to that place—
not the swallowing mouthfuls of pills
by the drinking fountain
next to my ninth-grade English class
one at a time, tiny sips of water, hoping to die.
I wanted every woman inside me
and I didn't even know what that meant.

The house was big and dark. Everyone moved out.
First the other family, then my grandparents, then my parents.
A shopping list of people left a freezer full of frozen burritos.
The lunchmeat drawer was stuffed with a ham too big to slice.

I wanted to be the weightless gun hidden
inside the typewriter, smuggled to the inmate.
What could it feel like to be that desired,
when the paid-off guard comes through the cell door,
all eyes fixed on the table where the typewriter is placed?

In the mental hospital, it was bright, and windy.
The sun shone on the newly painted white wall.
A boy sat next to me. It was as if someone smeared
the skin across his face. He wore white canvas high-top sneakers.
So did I.
He was the youngest at the county hospital.
I was the next youngest.
He was the only one there who'd tried to kill
someone other than himself.
In an afternoon he fell in love with me,
wanted to sit next to me in the dining hall at dinner.
I got out before dinner.
I copped a plea.
I gave away my plastic watch to the schizophrenic
with the rose tattoo on her wrist.

It wasn't hard to convince the psychiatrist,
who didn't give a shit, that I wasn't crazy.

Go to Alcoholics Anonymous, the nurse said.
Hours later my mother walked through the gates
and found me on the lawn playing, *Twinkle, Twinkle, Little Star*
on my harmonica for all the patients who sat around me in a
    circle.

At home that night I begged to keep wearing
the plastic hospital bracelet.
My mother made me cut it off.

Before the police hauled me off to the mental hospital,
I dreamt they would.
I was always being dragged off somewhere,
I just didn't know where yet.
I was going to funerals, I just didn't know whose.
I was crying for dead people and for the various places
I'd be held against my will.
It was half dream, half a wish
that I'd be removed from my life
where it was impossible to feel.
Or impossible not to feel everything.

In my head I'd live alone, in a small apartment.
I'd have tiny Christmas tree lights strung up in my kitchen

do you or don't you know
the two worlds I'm talking about,
the world that doesn't exist
where you wish you could be
on the dirt road that stretches out of Idaho
away from the cave and family?
The girl you want lives there.
You could take her on an inane date to the mall.
It doesn't always have to be the gun
smuggled inside the typewriter to the prisoner.
Or the prisoner's stomach that becomes the space
between jumping feet and the trampoline,

94

after they've smashed down
that air beneath them as they come up again.

All my life I've wanted to be the grand gesture
that forces the mouth open in disbelief.

Instead I was the lamp cord, collecting dust and never moving.
It's easy to be the destroyed one.
The big drip, the sullen runaway who won't leave
no matter how much you beg them to.
They only threaten, and then maybe,
they make a great escape to the neighbor's basement.

The trampoline throws a body back up in the air,
I'll draw you a picture,

here is the trampoline,
you've just jumped onto it
and here is how it throws you up
and the space here,

between the feet and the bottom of the trampoline,
that's where you fucked the air for the first time ever,

and you feel proud and light and without your brain.
Look—the harder you jump down,

the bigger the space,
it throws you off in joy,
it's not your fault that at some point you won't want to jump
    anymore,
your legs will tire and the space will evaporate
and tomorrow, the trampoline may be sold to buy groceries
or you may fall in love with someone who has a temper
and will stab it thirty times with a hunting knife,

but before that, remember—
the feeling of being catapulted,
keep this picture in your pocket, to remind you.

Immediately after I left the cave
I wanted to get back to you,
a myth of which you had no part

Somewhere in Idaho, a gas station sold a waitress a six-pack of
beer
and watched her drive her truck off into the six o'clock sun

I hadn't eaten all day,
the alcohol moved directly to my brain
it was a hundred degrees
three thousand miles from home,
and the tiny cloth that was the ground beneath my feet
was wet and tearing from my weight
when the overheating U-HAUL stopped and the family
that was moving across country got out and asked for directions,
I broke out my map of southern Idaho
and tried to help, *what you need to do is take this road here,*
I looked for a county on the map
that was named something blessed.
They didn't know I was drunk
or this was only my second day in Idaho
and thanked me generously
before they poured water into their smoking engine.
That's when I decided to go to JACKPOT, NEVADA.

I was looking for a sign
and there were many to choose from:

IMPEACH CLINTON

EXIT 12, THE LAND OF MAKE BELIEVE

(Christian campground with barking dogs)

MALONE'S RV (good mother/bad daughter) SUPER CENTER

DENNY's (bad mother/good daughter) NEXT EXIT

ALL YOU CAN EAT (bad daughter/good mother) $3.99

I want to tell you how the sun came through the windshield
and shone on my filthy face,
and how the green paint inside the truck was covered in dust
how the loose seatbelt beat into the metal of the truck door
from the rushing wind coming in the open window
and how Rorschach looked bored, scared, and perplexed all at
      the same time.
If not angels and magic lands then fast cars and beer and
      cheeseburgers.

Inside the motel room, hundred-degree heat,
no telephone, COURT TV blared in the background,
scratchy bedspread, unmatched motel furniture,
curtains drawn. The bathroom sink filled
with ice and 16-ounce cans of Budweiser,

I tried to write you letters on the silver manual typewriter,

the TV was tuned to the channel that gives information
about the local blood drive and the location where
to go on the one day a month
when driver's licenses are issued,
love songs play behind the orange television screen
where blue-typed announcements moseyed on by
one line at a time.

I wait until five o'clock for the prime rib special
eat it quickly and leave an enormous tip for the waitress
with the badly dyed blonde hair and broken arm,
then I walk across the street in the scorching heat
telling myself the whole time I shouldn't be gambling.

The roulette wheel hemorrhages in my brain
and I awake in the casino
to the smell of cheap industrial carpet
and old cigarette smoke.
I drink my free gin and tonics and hope:

2, 5, 8, 28, 29, BLACK, EVEN.

Gracelessly I move between the roulette wheel and the slot
    machines.
For more than seven hours I am afraid to leave the same slot
    machine.
I leave only when my bladder is so distended with urine
it's too painful to remain shifting my weight
and my stomach is too swollen for me to bend
over and pick up the quarters I'm drunkenly dropping on the
    floor.
In the bathroom mirror I stare at the black circles under my
    eyes,
and force a smile at myself.
I need a sharp piece of glass
to separate myself from the mocking face.

I tried to call Lamby from the aisle
of pay phones where gamblers call their lovers,
winners or losers, on the other end
the lovers and children hate them.

I wanted to be transported to a different time

the phone rings and rings

Lamby remember when,
our heads dipped backwards into that summer midnight

that summer, summer of needing
to be held summer

late June, the sticky pavement,
someone's wine dripping down my calf,
my dreams hidden keys under mats and potted plants

pick the stone up
that's a hiding place for a key

open the front door, throw the coffee table on its end
break the window—drink the last warm beer
in my broken refrigerator, leave the footsteps of your love
muddy through my house.

When I left the casino the sun was an hour from rising
I walked head down hoping no one from the motel
would see me and know I'd lost money.

Fumbling to get the key in the door
I heard Rorschach inside scratching and whining.
Sorry, Sorry, Sorry, I said
before letting her out behind
the motel parking lot to piss on the hill covered in rattlesnakes.

I slept for four hours and then headed to Vegas.

LAS VEGAS

I know you are reading this poem which is not in your
    language
guessing at some words while others keep you reading
and I want to know which words they are.
I know you are reading this poem listening for
    something, torn
between bitterness and hope
turning back once again to the task you cannot refuse.
I know you are reading this poem because there is
    nothing else
left to read
there where you have landed, stripped as you are.

—Adrienne Rich, "(Dedications)" from *An Atlas of the
Difficult World*.

You aren't old enough yet to figure out why your whole life
you've felt like something is missing, *but then it's like wham!*
the car door slams on your foot and you realize
you want your family to be proud of you, even
though you've gone away like birds go away in winter,
only to come back when flowers bloom
and you can prove to everyone
you've made a good life for yourself,
Ha! I succeeded.
I wanted to win a bunch of money
appear lucky, hide behind the couch
and when my mother walked in, jump up and shout
Surprise! throwing fistfuls of money
around my grandmother's apartment.

How to return to the family you've been away from for so long,
to step inside the doorway of that house?
The daughter doesn't want anyone who isn't her girlfriend
to touch her, not the mother, not the father

the daughter has always wanted
to ask her mother questions like this:

will my lovers disappear like sleek cats through the fence-gap at
      midnight
and their eyes that reflect orange in front of the headlights,
will those bright eyes look away from the years
that come quietly up the road?

The years drove them around in circles,
like two lost cabs.

The daughter wants to turn the past on its back like a turtle or a
      roach,
leaving those legs walking futilely through the air
cheering on those starved and paralyzed years.

The mother put her makeup on,
got ready for work, while cigarettes burned
down, one by one, in the chipped red ashtray.
The daughter stood beside the blaring alarm clock
and shook the mother's sleeping body
who worked sixteen hours a day
and called the daughter and son
from pay phones between jobs.

When the mother found the daughter on the lawn of the mental
      hospital
playing *Twinkle, Twinkle Little Star* on her harmonica
the mother couldn't believe it, because she was gone the years
      that led to it.

When they finally came together,
they came together as guilty mother and guilty daughter
and found there was nothing there to trade.

Dear Lamby,

I saw my mom and grandparents in Vegas. Rorschach ate an entire pineapple upside-down cake that my Aunt Lucrezia made while everyone was at church. I'd been gambling at the supermarket (they have slot machines everywhere here!), and when I got back to the house there were pineapple rings lying on the carpet and crumbs everywhere. I can't seem to get relaxed. Everyone's been asking for you. I lost most of my money at the Palace Station Hotel and Casino. My mom used to take us there when we were younger because they had a 99-cent silver dollar pancake breakfast. The day I left, I was hugging my grandmother goodbye and over her shoulder on the news I saw the Palace Station had been struck by lightning and caught on fire. A day late and a class-action settlement check too late. This morning when I was walking Rorschach, there was a girl across the street who had short black hair and your similar build. Rorschach started pulling at the leash and wagging her tail furiously. I kept saying, that's not Lamby, that's not Lamby.

xoxox

P.S. I stole my high school photo off the wall at my grandma's house. You're going to die when you see it!

I saw the pictures.
I look happy and clean twelve years ago.
That smiling face.
That long brown hair.
When I wished, it felt like a steel door
was being shoved down my throat.

My mother and I were two sticks
ticking side by side down a rain-filled gutter
sometimes crossing paths.

When we fell, we fell, two suitcases,
side by side from the bridge.

I was about two and a half hours outside Albuquerque when I
        spotted them.
I didn't know they were hitchhikers
thought they were in a different kind of trouble,
over a hundred degrees, a man waved his red baseball hat furi-
        ously over his head,
two women sat behind him against the hill that ran along the
        interstate.
I pulled over immediately, thinking them fleeing or stranded . . .
in my rearview mirror I saw the women scramble off the hill
and all three ran to where I'd parked.
The man, drunk, insisted on riding in front with me,
the haggard women climbed in back.

The man didn't know the women.
The women had been dumped on the roadside
by a jealous husband and had walked for hours
before they ran into the drunk who had insisted
they collaborate and try to find someone to take
the three of them.
He thought it would be easier to get a ride
if he was with two women, they said.

The drunk sat on the far side of the cab
and Rorschach sat in the middle on top of a few pieces of fruit
that my grandfather had given me when I left Las Vegas.
Later that night she licked her fur
continuously until I realized her hind legs were matted in
        banana.

I was to drop the man before we reached
Albuquerque at a music store.
He asked if he could have a little money
when we got there and then remained unmoving
until I leaned forward toward the ashtray
filled with coins.

I hated him for asking for money.
For demanding to sit in front.
For being drunk.
For using the stranded women to get a ride.

I opened the ashtray and handed him a few coins.
He got out and one of the women in the back climbed up front.
Rorschach still sat between us. In the rearview mirror
I could see the other woman take her glasses off
and stretch out in the back, trying to sleep.
We're trying to make our five o'clock shift.
Where do you work? I asked.
Fanny's Fried Chicken in Albuquerque.

She was the sister-in-law of the woman
in the back who'd been dumped off by the jealous husband.
I offered her some of my water and my sandwich.
She declined.

For hours we drove, the sister-in-law's eyes shut,
and head back. I felt trapped.
I'd never made the decision to pick up hitchhikers
but had to do it anyway after they'd all scrambled down
from the hill and run hopefully to the truck.
I wasn't afraid for my life
it was their obvious misfortune
that made me self-conscious.

When we arrived in Albuquerque they thanked me
again and I saw them walking down a street lined
by chain-link fence and stray dogs.
I had to piss badly but I drove on
afraid if I stayed, I'd run into them again a hundred feet up the
    road.
When I got to the first truck stop a safe distance away
I stopped. The gas station backed up to a field
and I walked Rorschach among the litter
customary to such secluded places:

used condoms, beer cans, old box springs.

The hitchhikers had stirred something inside me—
why had I wanted to get away from them so quickly?
I had wanted to get away from my family as well.

It was dusk.
I ate a hamburger and called Lamby
from the pay phone, on the third ring she answered.
For the first time in weeks, I heard her voice.

Hello.

Lamby?

Hello?

Lamby, it's me.

Is anyone there?

A man walked out of the truck stop and looked at me.
That pay phone sucks, he said.

I climbed into the back of the truck wanting my arms around
 her.
The shoes of loneliness paced around me, bored.
Something cold touched my wrist.
I moved the fold of sleeping bag and saw
the woman hitchhiker had forgotten her glasses.

I thought about how many shifts at Fanny's Fried Chicken
she'd have to work before she could afford a new pair.

I'd drive them back to Albuquerque
and find Fanny's Fried Chicken.
I'd be the big hero.
That thought quickly passed.

I was hours beyond Albuquerque now.

Lamby's voice. Hello. Hello.
I wanted to race back to her.
Everywhere I went, I raced.
I'd raced to leave BROOKLYN.
Then raced to find CAMUS.
Raced to surprise my family.
Then raced to leave them.

I was walled by red-dirt mountains
every living thing had a face
dried and cracked from the heat.

Dear Lamby,

Wish you were here, glad you aren't. We'd never make it before they filled in the other half of the equation. Alone, I could be anything—farmer, tomboy—with you next to me, they'd know.

When I heard her voice I felt forgiven and unhistoried,
like when we were first together and lunatics

I wanted that first date back
our heads dipping back
into that summer midnight
that summer of needing to be held summer.

Dear Lamby,

You will never believe me if I tell you that I passed another motel that had CERTAINTY IS A PRISON *on its marquee out front. I wonder if that is some sort of regional motel marketing strategy.*

xoxox

BROOKLYN

The difference between Despair
and Fear—is like the One
Between the instant of a Wreck—
And when the Wreck has been—

The mind is smooth—no Motion—
Contented as the Eye
Upon the Forehead of a Bust—
That knows—it cannot see—

—Emily Dickinson #305

I don't want love stories to ever end
especially love stories that have to do with me.

If you haven't figured it out by now
lesbians lead dramatic, complicated lives.

Before I went to Camus I cheated on Lamby.
We went to a sliding-scale couples counselor
who only helped us because we made fun of her.
We saved our sixty dollars a session and moved in together.

Upstairs our forty-year-old neighbor sold drugs
and had fifteen-year-old boyfriends

downstairs we moved slowly around each other
not gorgeously, but like the yellow
that slowly overtakes the leaf's edge.

I began to sort my life out by making lists:

Things To Say When We've Let Each Other Down

1. I don't know how to change from this monster I've become.

Somewhere small where no one dies
there are towns like this, my hometown,
where when finally the suicide happens
it feels like the only eclipse that century
people huddle on their porches with silent excitement
and look toward the sky—

what could it mean to be that bright,
then blacked out, girls who go to sleep girls
and wake up butterflies,
then butterflies turned prostitutes
and prostitutes turned crack-whores?

Out the front window,
the prostitutes scream at each other
later, it's always different
they stumble by drinking orange soda.

I walked Rorschach under the overpass
on the only street in the world,
the only block in the world
53rd St. between 3rd and 2nd Avenue.

I moved in with Lamby for a while after I lived on the farm. The way I love her is like the way I can't love a part of me. We waitress then come home exhausted at three in the morning. We have to walk the dogs on the filthy ice and try not to fall. She lives upstairs from an illegal strip club. When we come in the door, the coke-addict bouncer pokes his head out of the strip club and pets the dogs forever because he's so high. Her apartment is either too hot or too cold. It smells like wet dog hair and warm trash when you step in the front door. The reward on these bitter nights after walking the dogs and surviving interactions with the drug-addict bouncer is to come upstairs and watch the news. Our legs ache from delivering 200 cheeseburgers. The apartment is dark—three in the morning. We sit on the couch with the dogs, and I look over at her face lit up by the television. Her beautiful eyebrows—occasionally illuminated. She stares straight ahead at the black ocean. Fishermen come from all over the sea with their high-powered squid lamps and try to recover the dead.

We're shipwrecked, do you hear me, they've stranded us in this
	country
given us only things to buy and jobs to earn the money to buy
	them—

the shoes of the dead float on the surface

and we the people have sunk to the bottom
our eyes straining past that blue-green surface
where our own voices chatter in the air above,
and invisible birds with bleached ribcages
hang in the sky like angel-ornaments

like thumbtacks pushed in a map
marking each new city we sought.

They wanted me to abduct you, Peter.
Except they wanted me to do it
in the consensual way where no one gets hurt.

I wanted something different.
Something different I thought would come out
of doing the same thing again and again.

The shoes of the dead floated on the surface of the ocean
until some were plucked by the coast guard,
indexed and put into plastic bags.

Rorschach periodically wakes and drifts off,
her brown eyes: two portholes of a submarine
staring out at that infinite ocean of wishes.

The on and on winter, where one bitter day
is a king that overthrows the next.
If I could find my feet again
firmly planted on the pier,
that filthy dock,
in deserted living rooms
and the heated passenger side of the car
on those country roads
in that winter air.

I'll never come together like the wall that meets the other wall—
the walls meet because someone forced them together with nails
        and cement.

I walk from room to room forgetting my purpose.

My purpose, to change from stray stone
to sleeping water
that stray stones fall through.

Simple wants remain like the blood-stained asphalt
where the deer was run over by the semi-truck.

When the apartment above me got robbed,
I slept while amateurs took
two and a half hours to saw the door in half.

And when the house next door caught fire,
my body refused to crawl out of bed

the sirens came closer, red lights spun
around the base of the living room ceiling
until I woke and mumbled to Lamby,
Do you think it's our house that's on fire?

Months later, holding on to her
I asked her not to leave.
I needed her arms around me in case we got robbed
I needed her with me when the house caught fire
if the dogs were suddenly struck with sickness,
I'd need her to wake me, hand me my coat
cold from hanging so close to the window in winter . . .

To take off is the easy part
screech down back roads into new towns
where new kinds of lovers wait

innocently take off stores, the shaky gun barrel
pointed at the clerk

to take her clothes off, like she took off yours
slow, hands undoing buckles
as if they were belts on the dead.

Wait until you're old enough to have a real enemy.
If you accumulate lovers like lost socks, you'll end up with a few.
The enemy will stick around even when you can't remember
how your mouth moved red-black against his wife in the dark.

I've taken/token some pictures of myself
the filthy curtain pulled past the filthy glass,
I'm trying to jerk off
but I can't come or sleep because
the landlord's "show pigeons" coo too loudly.

I Know Why the Show Pigeon Coos.

Hours later, still naked beneath the dog-haired sheets
the day's light leaks in and out my fingerprints on the glass.

I want you to climb in the front window of my house like the mice
    do
that way you could see me in my bedroom trying to make myself
    come
when it finally happens, there are no fireworks,
instead it sounds as if I'm lifting a heavy box.

I'm drunk now, holding a drink crooked and spilling drops on my toes. Like three raindrops, they hit the leather and make that sound pup, pup, pup. What a storm didja hear it, the three-drop rainstorm? Did you hear the one about the rainstorm that only gave three drops? Pup, pup, pup. Wack Job. I was listening to WFAN 660 AM and when they don't broadcast baseball games they have people call in and talk about all the things that upset them in the sports world. Mostly the hosts cut everyone off and the caller doesn't get to talk after asking their initial question. One caller called Carl Everett a Wack Job. He used to play for the Mets. I asked him for his autograph once but he wouldn't give it to me. "They oughta get ridda him. He's a real wack job." That's what the caller said. A real wack job.

Things Peter and I Could Do on a Date

1. Listen to sports radio in the cave.

Pornography That Has Moved Me in This Lifetime

1. Racetrack Cruiser

No matter how badly the mice want to eat the dog food,
some days it's simply not on the floor.

I spend many hours thinking of ways to get rid of the mice.

Once I ate a pickle at my work
that had been sprayed with roach poison

the next day I worried   for hours

mice would crawl family member by family member
out of the hole next to the radiator
across my bare feet and I'd be too sick to move off the toilet.

To put my mouth onto another mouth
onto the strong tendons of the neck.
Tendons like twisted cables that hold up a bridge—
that confusion, lack of ambition, fear
and memory that keeps darting through my brain's field
like a frightened deer

Times I Was Suicidal When the Sun Made Me Feel Better

1. Location: 938 Geary St. #603. My first apartment
sixth-floor studio, Tenderloin, San Francisco, 1992.
I was trying not to drink, sleeping fourteen hours a day.
I woke up only to go to work as a waitress at the International
House of Pancakes. I was lying on my mattress
which was on the floor and looking out the windows
at the whole blue sky, because I was on the top
floor and I could see two things: the roof across the way,
and a sign that said, *JESUS IS THE LIGHT
OF THE WORLD*. It was all in neon.
I wanted to get up off my mattress and
bow to the toilet blue sky and sun. I had no revelations.
I stood and moved to the window where all that sunlight
       streamed in.
There was no screen, no bars, just six floors down—
sometimes I'd sit near the window and feel afraid, singing a two-
verse litany in my head that went, *What if I fell, what if I jumped?*
The fact is I would have taken the elevator
down and stepped in front of the 38 Geary bus if I'd wanted to
       do it,
but on this day the rattling object inside me,
settled into its place and stopped rattling, for an hour.
I sat on the windowsill, felt the sun on my face.

Some people are afraid of me
because they think I'm a hoodlum.
That I'm a punk on the corner who only menaces,
that's because I have so much anger even
when I pull my jacket tight around me the anger comes out
flapping its millions of small wings and perching on places
     under
my eyebrows, and on the faint, faint lines at the corners of my
     mouth.
And sometimes when Rorschach needs to be walked,
I don't have the energy to do it, and all I can do is lie in bed and
     count
the hours her disappointed face stares back at mine.
I need God. I need someone to take
that smell the air gets when it's summertime
and collect it in a scarf and put that scarf against my face so
     lightly
it smells like people living, like the sun got up in the sky and
     baked
the red dirt of the desert and then when the red dirt of the desert
got baked that smell got in the air and then people
had BBQs and bought Frisbees and didn't beat their wives for an
     afternoon,
an afternoon where everything wasn't so serious.
If we could do anything together I would want to listen to
     SPORTS RADIO.
It's truly fascinating. We could bring sandwiches into the cave
and you could see what I mean. People call in and say things
     like,
First time, long time, love your show, man.
"First time, long time" means they're calling for the first time
but they've listened for a long time.

Things That Make Me Feel Overwhelmed Every Day

1. I will always be an infidel.
2. The leak getting bigger in my ceiling.
3. Writing letters to Peter even though it's years later.

By the way, it's years later Peter.

I'm sure you're wondering how things ended,
were there any big car chases, impregnations. . . ?

Dear Lamby,

"And sometimes when we touch . . ." Boy is radio bad in the Midwest. It won't be long before I'm home now. I bought you the best souvenir. It's one of those cow legs that they hollow out and make into a flask for wine.

xoxox

Top Euphoric Groping Sessions

1. I forgot we'd made love for days
until she left and I saw the sheets covered in blood
and crumpled up in places where we pressed down
onto them and fumbled, heavy on top of the other.

That morning at the airport
I was too shy to look into her eyes.
After I threw her suitcase in the truck
we groped madly in the airport parking lot
she buttoned her pants when we stopped to pay
the parking attendant, I swerved home on the highway
her hands down my shirt.

Someone should start a business chauffeuring
new long-distance lovers from the airport
to their homes so they can fuck in the car.
She brought me the most exquisite bottle of gin.
It was nine in the morning, but we each had some
as she pulled a hundred sexy outfits from her suitcase.
When she pulled out the padded nightstick—I chuckled
nervously. This was her first time visiting me.

It's not the sex but something else
that happens in those rooms, where you let yourself
lie perfectly still
revealed yet deeply clothed.
Savor those 9 a.m. gin-drinking mornings,
they won't happen often enough, even though
while they're happening you believe you'll be smart enough
to make them a model for your life.

The pond is clear, the sun is directly overhead,
I'm not middle-aged or young,
I look through the clear water and see the tall algae stalks
    swaying

at the bottom of the pond are many stones,
most are not extraordinary, or even clean.

Dear Lamby,

Spent the night in Avoca, Iowa. My heel is killing me because a nail is coming through the sole of my shoe and digging into it. There are so many bugs here. They keep flying in through the air conditioner, then they dart around the room. I should have known when I unlocked the door and saw a flyswatter next to the phone and tiny writing tablet.

xoxox

P.S. I thought of the best name for a bar, the runaway waitress. We could give waitresses their first drink free.

My whole life I feared tomorrow would be less than today—
I know we're strangers, but hold me up.
This morning birds appeared and disappeared
in the long frost-covered stems,
I'm drinking coffee and Rorschach is curled up
on the bed, watching the birds dive and rise out the window.

The knife blade folds back and forth into itself.
The click-clack of sadness.

Dear Lamby,

Spent the night in the Diplomat Motel, in Elkhart, Indiana. Did you know Elkhart produces more than fifty percent of the nation's band instruments? I shut the curtains of the motel window so Rorschach couldn't see anyone outside and start barking. My foot hurts. The nail that holds the heel of my boot on has been stabbing me for weeks, but I can't bear to get rid of these boots because they're my favorites. I should be off before the motel people find out my cooler leaked and now their carpet is like the Red Sea. There is a pattern in the wood on the door that looks like Joan of Arc.

xoxox

For I will consider my dog Rorschach.
For she is the sanest one in this truck.
For her spots are organized and calm.
For when she bites people or dogs, she bites with willingness and
   duty.
For she glares dourly from the inside of twenty-eight-dollar
   motel rooms.
For she barks at every falling leaf.
For the superior manner in which she walks away from her bowl
   when I've filled it with beer.
For she has the face of God.
For her spots are innumerable and abundant.
For the one spot on her tail that barely made it and sits on the
   tip.
For her warm body to curl up to on cold nights in scary rest
   areas.
For her appetite is ceaseless.
For her zest of living exceeds her appetite.
For her joy in menacing smaller animals.
For her stealthiness in stealing food.
For she loves her life.
For her ears are the softest in the land.

Dear Lamby,

The whole way through Texas I kept seeing the same sign for a restaurant where if you eat an entire 72-ounce steak dinner—you get it for free. That's four and a half pounds! That's a premature baby! You have to eat the steak, baked potato and vegetables in order to get it for free. Can you imagine getting through the steak and the guy saying well there are a few carrots left on the plate . . . If you don't eat it all then you have to pay for it, and of course you can imagine how much a 72-ounce steak would cost.

At the Texas/Oklahoma border I saw red and blue lights flashing in my rearview mirror. I pulled over to the side of the road. It was hot and dry out and the wind was blowing dust every which way. The state trooper walked up to my truck in his ten-gallon hat and knee-high leather boots. It made me think about one of the first porn stories I'd ever read, when this cop pulls over this woman and handcuffs her hands above her head and forces her to have sex with him right there. When he knocked on the window, Rorschach went nuts.

"License and registration."

I tried to get it out of my back pocket. Rorschach was jumping over me and clawing at the window.

"Please step out of the car."

My shirt was stained with hamburger grease and I wasn't wearing a bra. I slipped out of the truck, locking Rorschach inside. He fumbled with my license and registration while asking me various questions over the noise of the four-lane highway.

"Would you mind stepping into the cruiser with me so I don't have to yell over this traffic?" he asked.

He's going to ask me for sexual favors in exchange for the ticket. I felt frightened and excited by the prospect of this. His car was air conditioned and smelled faintly of leather and breath mints. I looked at his crotch quickly.

"So, you're from New York, huh?" he said as he began to fill out my ticket.

I was sure he'd seen my out-of-state plates and tried to get me for whatever I was worth. I wasn't a speeder. Dust blew hard into the windshield of the cop car. I could see Rorschach's face in the side mirror of the truck—waiting for me.

"Do you know why I pulled you over," he asked.

"No," I said, looking at his crotch again.

"You were going 73 in a 70 mph zone. But that's not why I'm going to write you a ticket. I'm going to write you a ticket for not wearing your seat belt."

"Asshole," I thought. "I'm not sleeping with him now."

"What are you carrying in the back of the truck, got any contraband in there?"

"What's contraband?"

"Drugs, guns . . . dead bodies." He chuckled at his own joke.

"There's one dead body."

He looked at me, charmed by my sassy irreverence. He had patches of dry skin on his enormous knuckles. My stomach had the feeling it gets right before I gamble or take a large quantity of drugs not knowing whether they'll kill me.

"So what's that dead body smell like after it's been there a week?"

He was playing along. I looked at his crotch again.

I heard Rorschach bark. When I looked up I saw a cow had walked up to the edge of the fence and was staring at her through the truck window.

"It smells a little bit like a paranoid Dalmatian."

He handed me my ticket, chuckling.

"Make sure you wear your seat belt," he said.

I opened the car door and stepped out into the hot air.

His huge frame was crowded behind the steering wheel.

148

I almost forgot to ask him, "Have you ever eaten the 72-ounce steak?"

"Oh no, I can't finish that thing. A buddy of mine ate it all though. You know you got to eat the vegetables and potatoes too. Not just the steak. Why, you planning on going out that way?"

"No. I just keep seeing the signs."

xoxox

The ones who designed solitary confinement
knew what they were doing.

Did you know tollbooth employees
are more likely to commit suicide than any other occupational
    group?

Too much time and the dead deer on the side of the road scared
    me.
It had been slaughtered, its middle section removed.

I used to wake up early so I could wish.
My wishes were planets that didn't exist.
My wishes were horses the richest man couldn't afford.
Behind my dog's eyes rocks an infinite ocean of wishes.
I took jobs where I could be alone all day.
I delivered flowers and worked in cold, gray rooms filing.
All so I would have time to wish.

At my grandmother's house
as soon as I closed my eyes, I'd go into a different room.
And in that room the only thing that happened
is the man with the yellow eyes, tried to glare me down
or show me the time a hundred years ago
that he killed someone in the house I was living in.

At this moment I'm not afraid.
I'm tired, have an upset stomach half the day
and have a hard time putting my words in the right order.
People ask me for directions to get on a bridge
I have to go over every day, and I can't figure out how to tell them.

The heavy weight of me,
the wrought iron poles inside the wall,
the continuous chanting.

You, my children, who have been promised nothing
sent to build your own houses but given no wood or tools,

break what you need to break, throw the glasses
that were meant to be drunk from, one at a time into the wall
and watch them shatter, draw in your breath, as you do
when your clothes have been undone from your smooth
shining bodies, when you've been unable to see tomorrows
and the edges and shapes of them, undo your blindness
move your hands over the flat surface of the kitchen table
when you've sat like sheep ready to be examined before the sale.

Once, I found myself beneath a woman,
her legs straddled my lap, her face bent down
to my turned-up mouth, my turned-up mouth
that was turned like flames following the curve
of gasoline thrown by the arsonist.
I wanted exactly what happened that night
for this woman, to undo the buttons of my shirt
exactly as she did,
it was as if the shirt were my skin,

for months after, I was haunted by buttons
opening and falling like the light plunk of a penny
into a wishing well, there's no way I loved her,
and I know she's never even thought about those buttons
and how they felt, like something sacred,
like she was God and I was the dying child coming home.

I know what it feels like to have nothing to lose.
Looking over my shoulder on the dark street
Kill me if you're going to kill me motherfucker
I waited to be touched by the hand of God.
Who hasn't waited to be touched by the hand of God?
Still we have to buy our groceries
and be interesting lovers while we wait.

I'm stacking up my hope like small boxes, neat boxes
against the neat wall of the neat closet.

Thousands and thousands of drops,
country rain, when it rains and there's nothing around
for the rain to hit, no bus stop shelters
or groups of factory workers running up the street
with plastic bags tied over their heads.

I'm confused about the thing in us humans that's responsible for our rise or decline. I've seen ravaged faces. Ravaged beyond any of my own reflections. My rope's been cut and I've drifted. The next thing I know, I'm thirty blocks away, walking in the wrong direction. It feels so good to be alive. Even though sometimes I can't believe I'm still alive. I think we're like lions, wandering a field somewhere, oblivious to our strengths and beauty, never knowing a mirror or knowing what it means to have such golden—beautiful—fur

Once I wanted to sail down the street in a boat made of our
    laughter.

Once I held the dry end of my life's straw, between my lips.

Once I brought you my face, like a broken engine,
cradling its unbearable weight in my arms,
before putting it down on the floor of your garage.

Once I wanted to be the smuggled gun, hidden inside
the typewriter, taken into your jail cell, where you sat ready
to make the hard decision, right or wrong.

I wanted to be the movie star you would obsess over to forget
your boring life.

The hulking form of tomorrow
the neglected tenement I let myself become

the house I grew up in had walls without holes,
I hadn't seen the movies yet where people run off
to drafty garages with mattresses thrown on the floor
and drugs folded within plastic
and pushed deep down into damp pockets,
where lovers appear like God does, in a dream, long enough to
    say,
I'm here and I'm leaving.

I'm alive.
It's true.
Despite that I tried not to be.

When I was young I brought my rolls of pennies into the bank, and the teller threatened me, saying if there weren't enough pennies in the roll, my account would be deducted in accordance to how many coins were missing. I heard stories about people who put five pennies on each end of the roll and stuffed the middle with sand. That seemed like such an effort to try and cheat someone out of forty cents. In high school as a prank, someone Krazy-Glued a penny over every single lock and keyhole so none of the doors could be opened and the school was shut down for the day. I always thought that was smart. I love how it takes so much to destroy a penny.

Wrap the years of being lost around your knuckles,
like a frayed sweatshirt and punch out the window
of your future—

the raft dips up and down
edging farther and farther away
then comes back into sight,

I always come back to the same things in life,
wanting women to love me, and men to love me,
and stray dogs to love me, and then thousands more.

I forgot how desire stitch by stitch
undoes the flesh of legs.

Some don't want luck to come flittering in:
a kid brought a machete to school and cut the other kid.

At school, kids beat up the principal twice.
They beat him until he quit being the principal.

I stood far away from them all.
I tried to do my job.
I stood far away and could smell them
cooking food from my childhood.

It's hard to explain the passion that baseball fans feel when watching a game. Once I went to a game in a black sequin mini-dress and purple feather boa. I had a huge sign that said JOHN OLERUD ELOPE WITH ME. He was the first baseman for the New York Mets. Unlike Carl Everett, he's not a WACK JOB, and he gave me his autograph when I was drunk and hanging over the dugout after a game. He's very polite. I know it must be hard to believe I'm gay since I always talk about men. It's hard rooting for one team to hit a white ball the size of a fist that's traveling almost 100 mph "out of the park." "Out of the park" usually means over 400 feet. That's a lot of pressure to hang the mood or tone of your day on the improbability of such a thing. But when it happens, God. It's like you're the one person that fell from the fiery plane into the ocean and lived.

Once I only believed in beginnings,
my wishes were horses the richest man could never afford
my wishes were planets that never existed
my wishes were elements that refused to coincide,

I wanted to be virgin body against virgin body.

When I first loved, I loved like a lunatic
my socks embroidered with thorns and pine needles
the bottom of my lungs, tiny flight fires.

I wanted those days back even if I had to shove a gun
square into memory's temple and demand them

you will mourn the loss of lunatic love
whether or not you miss the lunatic or the lunatic misses you.

When the police dragged me to the mental hospital,
part of me was happy.
Happy that a file somewhere said:
I'm so sad, I ended up here.
My proof.

Once I only knew how to show you dead things:

mourning families who hold the heavy stone
the uncomfortable animal with no name in their bellies
and wander from room to room,

whole families killed in devastating earthquakes,
in cars on slick roads at night
in the hands of love's imposter cousin
with firearms and hatchets,
with police weapons,
with the his and her badges on the nightstand.

When there is only half a breath of daylight left
like the second between when you think you're sleepy
and when you shut your eyes is when those hundred curves
of every leaf step to the side and let the orange come over the
    horizon,
the mute/prodigy sunset
this hermit waves its arms across the sky,
the light, one very gentle brush stroke across—
like a telephone cord leading somewhere . . .
our eyes follow it to the blowing horn of an unseen train . . .
we look to where it should be,
find nothing but the outline of a small-town grocery
and now with almost no breath of light left
we look down on our hands.

Ali Liebegott is the author of the award-winning books *The Beautifully Worthless* and *The IHOP Papers*. In 2010 she took a train trip across America interviewing female poets for a project titled, *The Heart Has Many Doors* — excerpts from these interviews are posted monthly on *The Believer Logger*. In addition, she is the founding editor at Writers Among Artists whose first publication, *Faggot Dinosaur*, was released in 2012. Her most recent novel, *Cha Ching!* was published by the City Lights/Sister Spit imprint in 2013.

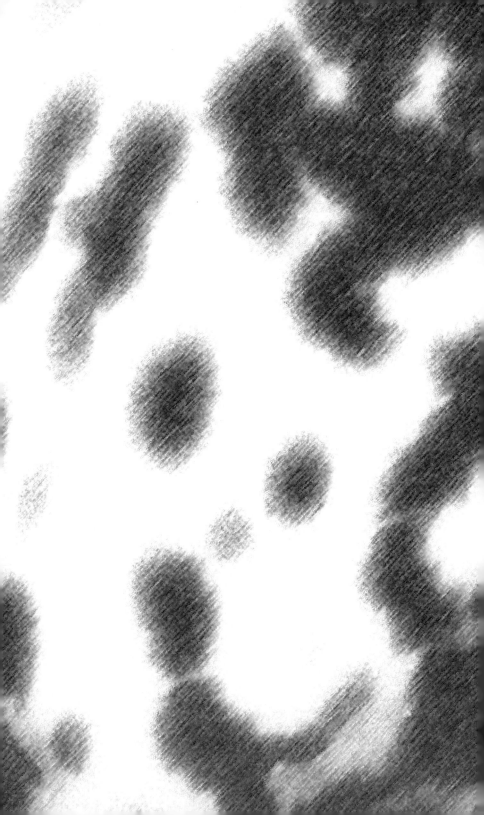